dick brun

GW00402273

miffy
at the
play-
ground

SIMON AND SCHUSTER
London New York Sydney Toronto New Delhi

One day Father Bunny said –

We're going out today.

Let's spend it at the playground.

Oh good, cried Miff. Hooray!

They had to go by car, because

the playground was so far.

But Father Bunny said at last,

right then, here we are.

Oh yes, said Miffy. I can see.

This park has everything.

I wonder what to go on first?

I think I'll try the swing.

Look at Miffy swinging here,

holding with each hand.

She could have swung while sitting down

But Miff preferred to stand.

Then on the rings, oh that was fun,

Miff went to and fro.

It felt so good that Miffy thought,

I'll have another go.

Clever Miffy span around

the horizontal bar.

Mother was impressed and said,

Miffy, you're a star!

And then there was a climbing tree

which Miffy thought she'd try.

It was a little scary –

but fun to go so high.

Next she took a turn upon

the smooth and slippy slide.

It feels like flying, Miffy called.

It's such a speedy ride.

Oh, look, a seesaw, Father said.

Shall we have a try?

Miffy laughed when Father's weight

kept her stuck up high.

And do you know what else there was,

this blue thing on the green?

A thing for jumping up and down on,

yes – a trampoline.

When Miffy had tried everything

Mother said – I think

it's nearly time to head for home,

but first a juicy drink!

Then Miffy's father said, jump in.

It's time to go. Beep-beep!

What a lovely day, said Miffy.

Then . . . she fell asleep.

original title: nijntje in de speeltuin
Original text Dick Bruna © copyright Mercis Publishing bv, 1975
Illustrations Dick Bruna © copyright Mercis bv, 1975
This edition published in Great Britain in 2015 by Simon and Schuster UK Limited,
Publication licensed by Mercis Publishing bv, Amsterdam
English translation by Tony Mitton, 2015
ISBN 978-1-4711-2332-0
Printed and bound in China
A CIP catalogue record for this book is available from the British Library upon request
10 9 8 7 6 5 4 3

www.simonandschuster.co.uk